The Abandoned Puppy

Pet Rescue Adventures:

Also by Holly Webb:

The Abandoned Puppy

by Holly Webb
Illustrated by Sophy Williams

tiger tales

5 River Road, Suite 128, Wilton, CT 06897
Published in the United States 2018
Originally published in Great Britain 2007
by the Little Tiger Group
Text copyright © 2007 Holly Webb
Illustrations copyright © 2007 Sophy Williams
ISBN-13: 978-1-68010-091-4
ISBN-10: 1-68010-091-2
Printed in China
STP/1800/0152/0817
All rights reserved
10 9 8 7 6 5 4 3 2 1

For more insight and activities, visit us at www.tigertalesbooks.com

Contents

For Kitty

Chapter One
A Real Treat

The littlest puppy whimpered quietly. The cardboard box had stopped bouncing up and down, but no one had come to get her out, and it was still so dark. She didn't like it. She didn't know where her mother was, and she was hungry.

She squeaked in frightened surprise as a low rumbling noise shook the box. It seemed to be moving again, swinging and then sliding across the floor. Her two brothers slammed into her, knocking her against the side of the box as the car went around a sharp corner.

The journey seemed to go on for a very long time, but she couldn't even curl up to sleep. Every time she managed to get comfortable, the box would slide around again, and they'd all be on top of each other. It was nothing like their rough-and-tumble puppy play in the big basket at home. This hurt, and they couldn't go and snuggle up against their mother when they wanted the game to stop.

Pressed into the farthest corner, the puppy scratched anxiously against her brothers. They were sitting on her again! Then she realized that they'd stopped— the box wasn't sliding around anymore. Her brothers stood up cautiously. They listened, flinching a little at the creaky wheeze of the car trunk opening. Then the box swung up into the air and was dropped down with a heavy thud.

They heard footsteps hurrying away. And then they were left alone.

"Are you ready to go, Zoe?" Aunt Jo was standing at the front door of their house, wearing her rain boots and her Redwood Animal Rescue fleece.

"Yes!" Zoe dashed down the hallway, stuffing the packet of dried apricots that Mom had found in the back of the cupboard into her lunchbox. She and Mom had both forgotten she'd need packed lunches this week, so Zoe's lunch was a bit random. Still, she really liked peanut butter and jelly sandwiches!

"Where's your older sister?" Aunt Jo asked, peering down the hallway into the kitchen.

"She's still asleep." Zoe shook her head. "Kyla thinks I'm crazy to get up early to come with you when I don't have to."

"Well, if you stayed at home with your sister all day, you'd just end up watching TV for the entire Easter vacation!" Mom called out. "You'll have a much better time at the shelter!"

"I heard that!" Kyla's voice floated down from upstairs. "I'm not asleep, and I'm not watching TV. I'm studying! In bed! See you later, Aunt Jo. I'll come and pick Zoe up."

Kyla had exams coming up, so she was studying as hard as she could. Zoe was really glad that Aunt Jo had said she could help out at the rescue—she normally only got to help out after school. It would have been boring being stuck at home with

Kyla, and Mom couldn't afford to take
any time off work. Sometimes when
they were off from school, she got
to spend the day with her friend Becca,
but Becca had gone to her grandmother's
in Canada for two weeks.

"Thanks for letting me come for the
entire day," Zoe said to Aunt Jo as they
walked to the rescue, which was about
10 minutes from Zoe's house.

"That's all right!" Aunt Jo grinned at
her. "I'm not going to be letting you off
lightly, you know. I've got a long list of
jobs for you to do, starting with cleaning
out the dogs' runs, then bathing the
cats, and maybe even knitting some
bodywarmers for the guinea pigs...."
She looked down at Zoe's worried face.
"I'm just teasing you, Zo! There will

be a lot of useful stuff you can do, I promise, but it'll be mostly exercising the dogs, if it's not too wet. They don't get walked as much on the weekends, because that's when we get most of our visitors. They'll all be desperate for a good run around the yard."

Redwood was a small rescue, but it took in every kind of animal. The staff did their best to get them all adopted, but it wasn't always easy. Aunt Jo had been working there for three years now, ever since she'd gone to the rescue to get a cat and come home with Boots, her handsome tabby. She had been working as a receptionist at the local vet back then. That's how she knew all about Redwood. She'd ended up volunteering to help out at the rescue in her spare time. Then, when a job had come up as manager, she'd jumped at the chance. Zoe had been delighted, too.

"You're so lucky, getting to be at the rescue every day, and seeing all the dogs," Zoe sighed. "I'm definitely going to work somewhere like Redwood when

I'm older. Or maybe I'll be a vet," she added thoughtfully.

Aunt Jo smiled at her. "It's a great job at the rescue," she agreed. "But it does have its downsides, too. Sometimes it makes me so angry the way people don't take care of their animals properly. And it isn't always the owner's fault, either. Sometimes they really love their pets, but they just can't take care of them in the same way anymore. That's really heartbreaking." She sighed. "I just want to take them all home with me. But four cats is enough!"

Having just Boots the tabby hadn't lasted very long. Aunt Jo was a softie when it came to big fluffy cats.

"So, did anybody take a dog or cat home over the weekend?" Zoe asked.

She loved hearing about the new homes the animals went to. She liked to imagine herself into some of the stories Aunt Jo told. She would love to have a dog from the rescue, but she knew they couldn't. It wouldn't be fair to leave it all alone in their house while Mom was at work, and Kyla wasn't really a dog fan, either. She'd been chased across the park by a huge Bernese mountain dog when she was about four years old. She and Mom had been on their way to preschool, and Kyla had been on her scooter. The dog had only wanted to be friendly, but Kyla hadn't known that, and she'd fallen off trying to get away from him. She'd been scared of dogs ever since.

"Eddie got chosen this weekend!"

said Aunt Jo. "Finally! I'm so happy, Zoe. I thought he'd never find a home!"

Zoe grinned. Eddie was one of the older dogs—a bulldog. A lot of people seemed to think that they were weird-looking. Everyone always wanted a cute little puppy, but Eddie had such a sweet nature.

"An elderly man came in," Aunt Jo went on. "He wanted Eddie right away. He said that he'd always had bulldogs, and Eddie was perfect. One of the staff did a home visit, because Mr. Johnson was so eager to take Eddie right away. She said it looked ideal. A nice yard, and near a park for good walks. She figured Eddie and Mr. Johnson were a perfect match—both of them being on the elderly side. You know Eddie never liked walking very fast!"

Zoe giggled. She'd taken Eddie around the park with Aunt Jo and a couple of the other dogs from the rescue before. It was the slowest walk she'd ever been on!

"Lucky Eddie. And lucky Mr. Johnson," Zoe said. "I bet they're having such a great time." She wrapped her arm through Aunt Jo's and leaned against her with a sigh. "I know we can't, but I wish I could have a dog of my *own*...."

Chapter Two
The Nighttime Delivery

The box seemed to be getting colder and colder. The April night had been frosty, and the puppies had huddled together to keep warm. They weren't used to being outside at night, and there was only the thin cardboard box between them and the concrete steps. They had always slept in their comfortable basket, snuggled up next to their mother. The cold was a frightening shock.

The smallest of the three, the tiny girl puppy, woke up first. She was miserably stiff, the cold aching inside her, and she scratched worriedly at the cardboard under her paws. Her two brothers were still asleep, curled up together, but somehow during the night she had rolled away from them. Now she was on her own in the corner of the box, shivering and hungry.

She tried to scratch at the side of the box, wondering if she could get out, and somehow find her way back to her mother.

But even her claws hurt this morning, and she felt weak and sleepy. Too feeble to claw a hole in the side of a box.

She still didn't understand what had happened. Why had they been taken away from their mother, and their warm basket? Was someone going to come and get them, and take them back to her? When they'd been put into the box, she'd heard her mother barking and whining—she hadn't wanted them to go any more than they had. The littlest puppy had a horrible feeling that they might not be going back.

Zoe and her aunt were almost at the rescue. Zoe could feel herself speeding up. She loved it when they got to be the ones who opened up at Redwood— it was a real treat and usually only happened if Aunt Jo let her come and help on a Saturday. She knew that all the animals would be excited to see someone after a night on their own. The dogs would be the most obvious about it, jumping around and scratching at the wire mesh on the front of their pens, and barking like crazy. But even the cats, who usually liked to be more standoffish, would spring up from their baskets and come to see who was there. The rescue had a big pen full of guinea pigs at the moment, so there would be happy squeaking from them, too.

Aunt Jo was searching in her bag for the keys, so it was Zoe who first noticed that there was something strange on the front steps.

"What's that?" she asked curiously, frowning at what looked like a box in front of the main door to the rescue.

Aunt Jo looked up from the bunch of keys. "What?"

"There. On the steps. Maybe someone donated food to the shelter, Aunt Jo!" People did bring in pet food for the animals occasionally—Zoe had seen them. "It's funny that they didn't bring it in when there was someone who could say thank you, though."

"Hmmm…." Aunt Jo was walking faster now, the keys dangling forgotten in her hand.

24

"What's the matter?" Zoe asked. She could see that her aunt looked worried.

"People leave us other things, too, Zoe," Aunt Jo sighed. "It might be an abandoned animal in that box. If it is, I guess that at least they've brought it to us, but I hate it when they just leave it like that."

Zoe felt her eyes filling with tears. The box was just a box, a shabby cardboard one. How could someone stuff a cat or a dog in there, and then just leave it? It was so mean!

They hurried up the steps and sat down slowly, one on either side of the box. Aunt Jo took a deep breath. "I never get used to this," she whispered as she started to unfold the flaps on the top. "It's been such a cold night. Look, there's frost on the top. If there's something inside, I hope it hasn't been in there for long."

There was a feeble scratching noise from inside the box, and Zoe caught her breath. "There *is* something inside there!"

Aunt Jo frowned at the box. "Yes.

And I'm being silly, Zo. We should take the box inside. We don't want whoever's in here getting scared and leaping out."

Zoe nodded. "Good idea. Can I take it?" she asked hopefully. "You can unlock the door."

Carefully, Zoe slipped her hands underneath the box, shivering as she touched the clammy, cold cardboard. Whoever was in it must have had a miserably cold night. She heaved the box up and felt something inside it wriggle.

There was a worried little squeak, and a yap.

"It's okay," she whispered. "We're just taking you into the rescue. It'll be nice and warm in there. Well, warmer than out here, anyway."

Aunt Jo had unlocked the doors now, and she was just turning off the alarm. She held the door open for Zoe, and they hurried into the reception area, putting the box down on one of the chairs.

"I think it's a dog," Zoe told her aunt. "I definitely heard a yapping noise. But it can't be a very big dog, because the box hardly weighed anything at all."

"Let's see." Aunt Jo lifted the flaps of the box—it was meant to hold packets of chocolate cookies, Zoe noticed—and they both peered in.

Staring anxiously up at them were three tiny brown and white puppies.

Chapter Three
New Surroundings

The littlest puppy flinched back against the side of the box. She was still so tired from being bounced and shaken around, and now the light was flooding in, after hours of being shut in the dark. It hurt her eyes, and she whimpered unhappily. Her bigger, stronger brothers recovered more quickly, bouncing up to see what was happening, and where they were. But the little girl puppy pressed her nose into the corner of the box, hiding away from the light. She was too cold and tired to get up anyway.

Zoe and her aunt gazed inside, and Zoe pushed her hand into Aunt Jo's. She'd never seen such little puppies at the rescue. They were the smallest puppies she'd ever seen anywhere.

"Oh my goodness, three of them," muttered Aunt Jo.

"They're so tiny," Zoe whispered. "They can hardly weigh anything at all."

Aunt Jo nodded. "They're much too young to be away from their mother, really. They can only be a few weeks old. Great job keeping quiet, Zo. We don't want to scare them. They may not be used to seeing different people."

The puppies were looking up at Zoe and Aunt Jo uncertainly. One of the boy puppies scratched hopefully at the side of the box, clearly wanting to be lifted out.

"Well, he's not shy," Aunt Jo laughed quietly.

Very gently, she slipped her hands into the box and lifted out the puppy. He wagged his stubby little tail and licked her fingers. "Yes, you're a sweetheart, aren't you?" She turned to Zoe.

"They must be starving if they've been in this box all night. Now that I can see him clearly, I don't think this little boy can be more than four weeks old. He's probably only just been weaned from his mother. They should be having four or five meals a day, and a bit of their mom's milk still."

Zoe giggled. "That's why he's trying to eat your fingers...." Then she looked worriedly down into the box. "Aunt Jo, what about the little puppy in the corner? Is she okay? She isn't moving like the other two."

Her aunt sighed. "No, she isn't.... We'd better take a look at her. Can you bring the box into one of the puppy pens? Then we'll have somewhere cozy for them to curl up, and we can mix up some puppy milk."

Zoe gently lifted up the box, with two puppies still in it, and followed her aunt through to the main rescue area, where all the pens were. Dogs jumped up excitedly as they came past, barking for their breakfast, and for someone to come and give them some attention. Zoe looked down worriedly at the two puppies in the box. The bigger one—she was pretty sure it was another boy—was now standing up, balancing carefully on plump little paws, and listening to the new and exciting noises. He looked up curiously at Zoe—the only person he could see at the moment.

Maybe he thinks it's me barking! Zoe thought to herself, smiling down at him.

34

But her smile faded as she looked over at the other puppy. The tiny puppy was still curled miserably in the corner of the box. She didn't seem to want to get up and see what was going on at all.

"We'll put them in here—nice and close to the kitchen," Aunt Jo said, opening one of the pen doors, and crooning to the puppy snuggled in the crook of her arm. "I'm pretty sure we've got a big tin of that powdered puppy milk replacement left," Aunt Jo continued. "And some of the bottles. I'd better order some more, though."

She sat down on the floor in the pen with the puppy in her arms, and Zoe put the box down next to her, kneeling beside it. "Should we take the others out?" she asked, looking at the boy puppy, who was clawing excitedly at the side of the box now.

Aunt Jo nodded. "Be careful though, Zoe. Don't scare them. They might not be very big, but puppies can still nip if they're frightened. Get the bigger puppy out first, then we can let him explore with this one, while we see what's the matter with the tiny one."

Zoe reached in and picked up the puppy, who was still standing up against the side of the box. He wriggled and yapped excitedly, and when she put him down on her lap, he squirmed around eagerly, trying to see everything in the pen. Then he nuzzled Zoe's fingers, and wriggled carefully down the leg of her jeans, making for the floor. He obviously just wanted to go exploring in this new place.

The other boy puppy was still snuggled on Aunt Jo's lap, looking around curiously, but not quite confident enough to go marching around like his brother.

"Try just giving the little one a gentle pet," Aunt Jo advised. "Don't go right in and pick her up. She isn't looking at us, and she'd get startled."

Zoe reached in and ran one finger down the puppy's silky back. The brown fur was so soft, but she didn't feel as warm as her brother. "She's pretty cold," Zoe said, glancing at Aunt Jo. "Even just touching her. And she's sort of floppy."

Aunt Jo bit her lip. "She's suffered more being out all night because she's smaller. Here, put this on your lap, Zoe." She lifted a soft fleece blanket out of a padded basket in the corner of the pen. "Then lift her out carefully, and wrap her up. Just loosely. And keep your hands around her to warm her up a bit."

Zoe nodded, and gently cupped one hand around the puppy. The tiny dog shivered a little as she felt Zoe's fingers, and turned her head slightly. But she was just too weak to look up. Zoe slipped the other hand underneath her and lifted her out onto the blanket. She wrapped it around the puppy, petting her gently through the folds.

"Okay, little one," Aunt Jo said to the puppy on her lap. "I need to go and get your sister a hot-water bottle. And make some milk for you guys. Hmm?

Want to go and see this nice basket?" She put the puppy in and petted him for a few seconds until he got used to being somewhere new. Then she got up slowly. The other boy puppy trotted over to the basket, too, nosing affectionately at his brother.

"Those two seem fine," she said, sounding relieved. "And I'm sure they'll be even brighter once they've had something to eat."

Zoe looked up at her. "What about this one?" Her voice wobbled. "You don't think she's going to be all right?"

Aunt Jo sighed. "We don't know yet. She seems very weak. I'm going to call Samantha at the vet and ask if she'll come over as soon as she can and take a look at them all. Are you okay with them for a minute while I get a hot-water bottle for the little one?"

Zoe nodded, still gently rubbing the puppy through the blanket. She wished she could feel her moving. The puppy felt like a saggy little beanbag, slumped on her lap. Carefully she moved the blanket from around the puppy's head, looking at her face. Her eyes were closed, and her pink tongue was slightly sticking out of her mouth. *It looks dry,* Zoe thought worriedly. Aunt Jo had better hurry up with that puppy milk. She hoped they'd be able to persuade the puppy to drink it. She didn't look like she wanted to make the effort to do

41

anything at the moment.

"Here's the hot-water bottle," Aunt Jo said, hurrying back. "I've wrapped it up so it isn't too hot."

"Do we put her on top of it?" Zoe asked, starting to lift the puppy off her lap.

"No, that would be too hot. I'm going to put it at the side of the basket, then she can snuggle next to it. We'll just have to keep an eye on her brothers and make sure they don't nudge her away."

"Maybe we should put her in a pen of her own," Zoe said doubtfully. "They're a lot bigger than she is. They might push her around."

"I'd rather keep them together if we can. She's already lost her mother, and her home. Her brothers are the only security she knows. Also, if we separate her, she might find it difficult to manage being around other dogs when she's bigger."

Zoe nodded as she laid the puppy close to the hot-water bottle. "We don't want her to be lonely," she agreed.

"I've started to warm up some puppy milk. I'll just go and get it, and we can see what they think." Aunt Jo ducked into the kitchen and came back with a shallow metal tray of the special puppy milk. "Hopefully they won't tip this over," she explained to Zoe, who was looking at the tray in surprise—it looked like something her mom would make brownies in.

The two boy puppies had been nosing

43

around the edges of the pen, trying to explore, but as soon as Aunt Jo put the tray down, they galloped over to see what it was—so fast that they got tangled up and fell over each other. They struggled to their feet, mock-growling, and then scurried up to the tray, sniffing at it excitedly. It only took seconds before they were eagerly lapping, burying their tiny muzzles in the milk and splashing it around.

"They must have had milk from bowls before," Zoe said, watching them and giggling.

"Maybe. Or else they're just fast learners," said Aunt Jo. "I don't think we need to worry about them not eating." But she was frowning. "I'd really hoped that the smell would wake the little one up, but she doesn't seem to have noticed. We'll have to try feeding it to her by the bottle."

Zoe nodded. "Should I put her on my lap?" she asked hopefully. She'd loved holding the puppy before, and trying to warm her up. Even though it was frightening that the puppy was sick, it felt really special to be the one trying to make her better.

"Yes. Unwrap her, and we'll try to

get her to take a bottle. I brought one just in case." Aunt Jo took a baby's bottle with a cap out of the pocket of her fleece, and sat down next to Zoe. "She's still so sleepy...."

The puppy was really floppy now, and she didn't wriggle when Zoe unwrapped her. Aunt Jo held the teat of the bottle up to her mouth, but she didn't seem to notice it. She certainly didn't start sucking, as Zoe had hoped she would. She only turned her head away a little, as though Aunt Jo nudging the bottle against her mouth was annoying.

"She doesn't want it," Zoe said worriedly. "Is there anything else we can give her?"

"We could try using a syringe...,"

Aunt Jo said thoughtfully. "We can poke it into the corner of her mouth and try and trickle it in." But Zoe could see that her aunt was doubtful about the puppy ever feeding at all.

"What about…." Zoe brushed her fingers against the teat, letting a few drops of milk ooze out of the tiny hole onto her fingers. It was thick and yellowish, not like ordinary milk at all. Holding her breath, she moved her milky fingers across the puppy's mouth, letting the milk run onto the dry, pink tongue.

The puppy shivered with surprise, and the little tongue darted out, licking Zoe's fingers.

"She likes it!" Zoe squeaked.

Aunt Jo smiled. "You take the bottle. Squeeze a little out onto the end of the teat and dribble it into her mouth."

The puppy licked eagerly at the teat this time, and when Zoe pushed it gently against her mouth, she sucked, harder and harder, until she was slurping messily at the milk.

And then, at last, she opened her dark eyes and stared up at Zoe.

Chapter Four
Puppy Playtime

To: Becca
From: Zoe
Subject: Puppies

Hi Becca!

I hope you're having a good time at your grandmother's. I'm sorry I haven't emailed you in a couple of days. Been sooooo busy! I went to the rescue with Aunt Jo on Monday, and someone had abandoned three puppies in a box on the front steps!!! (Here's a picture.

Aunt Jo took it on her phone. Aren't they beautiful?) We've called the two boys Brownie and Chip and the girl puppy Cookie. She's really pretty. When we first found them, she was really weak, and Aunt Jo told me afterward she wasn't sure she was going to make it. We're giving her milk from a bottle because she won't eat mashed-up puppy food and milk, even though her two brothers love it! (You should see them eating. It goes everywhere, and we have to wash them afterward!) But some of it must be going inside them—they're getting fatter every day! Cookie is definitely getting bigger, too, and she likes me to carry her around everywhere! I have a bunch more pictures that Mom printed out for me, so I'll show you when you get back.

Love, Zoe xxxxxxxxxxxxx

To: Zoe
From: Becca
Subject: Re:Puppies

I can't believe you found puppies! You are so lucky. Grandma's place is okay, but it's a little cold since it's by the sea. I went swimming and my toes almost fell off.

Will the puppies get new owners from the rescue? How old are they? I wish I could come and see them. Guess what? Mom and Dad say we can definitely have a dog (you know they wouldn't make up their minds before). But now they say we have to go slow and make sure we find the right dog! Aaargh! I really want to have a dog NOW! When I get back please ask your aunt if I can come and see the puppies. Maybe one of them could be our dog!!!

Love, Becca xxxxxxxxxxx

Zoe read Becca's reply to her email, smiling to herself. Becca wrote emails just like she talked. But her smile faded a little as she read on to the end. Becca was so lucky to be allowed to have a dog. Zoe had been talking to Aunt Jo about the puppies today at the rescue. They'd been weighing them to check that they were eating enough, which was difficult because Brownie, Chip, and Cookie saw no reason why they should stand still on top of the scales, and just kept bouncing around. In the end, Aunt Jo had made a guess at their weights, but she said they were definitely getting heavier, which was the main thing.

Then they'd taken five minutes just to play with the puppies—it seemed like fun, rather than work, but Zoe knew it was actually really important. If the puppies didn't ever get played with, they wouldn't know how to behave with their new owners.

"How could anyone have abandoned them?" Zoe said sadly, watching Brownie and Chip zooming up and down the pen, chasing after a ball. Cookie was scampering after them, not quite brave enough or fast enough to take the ball from her brothers, but having just as much fun. "They're so perfect, all of them. How could anyone be so mean?"

Aunt Jo sighed. "Well, at least they brought them here. It was a start."

"But they left them out in the cold all night!"

"Some people just don't think. The puppies were probably an accident— they hadn't had the mom spayed, and then maybe the owners felt they couldn't afford to buy all the puppy food, and take the puppies to the vet for vaccinations. Dogs are expensive to own." She reached over to put her arm around Zoe's shoulders. "Don't think about it, Zo. The puppies were lucky they ended up here, so they've got all of us taking care of them. We're going to turn them into well-behaved dogs and make sure they only go to wonderful owners. They won't remember their horrible start."

"I hope not," Zoe whispered, with a tiny sigh. Aunt Jo's words were meant to make her feel better. She knew the puppies would need to leave the rescue in a few weeks, but she'd been trying not to think about it too much. She'd only known them for a few days, but they were so sweet,

Cookie especially. If they could stay at the rescue for a little longer, she'd be able to keep taking care of them…. But that wasn't fair. They needed forever homes.

Reading the exciting news in Becca's email had made her think about having to say good-bye to the puppies all over again….

To: Becca
From: Zoe
Subject: Puppies

Hi Becca,

Aunt Jo thinks the puppies were about four weeks old when we found them, so now they're five weeks. They can't go to new homes until they're about eight weeks old. I'm sure you can come and see them! I'll ask Aunt Jo. You're so lucky to get a dog! I hope your mom and dad decide on one soon. See

you back at school in a week!

Love, Zoe xx

It wasn't as friendly as her emails to Becca usually were, but Zoe was feeling sad. She stared at her computer screen, not really seeing the cute photo of Cookie that she had set as her wallpaper.

"What's up?"

Zoe jumped. She hadn't heard Mom come in at all. "Nothing…. I was just thinking about the puppies. I'm going to miss them so much when they get adopted." She gulped. "Especially Cookie."

Mom nodded. "She is beautiful." Zoe had shown Mom the puppies one afternoon at the shelter when Mom had come to pick her up. "I think it's her eyes. She has such a little face that it makes her eyes look huge, and then she has those beautiful whiskery eyebrows. Has Aunt Jo figured out what breed they are yet?"

Zoe giggled and shook her head. "Nope. Everyone at Redwood thinks they're something different. Aunt Jo thinks maybe there's some Jack Russell in them and maybe some Cockapoo, too. But we might not be able to tell until they're bigger. Almost grown-up. And we won't have them then, will we? So we'll never know." She sniffed, and Mom hugged her.

"But you knew they'd have to go to new homes, Zo! All the animals at the rescue do. You've never gotten this upset before."

"I know. Maybe it was because we found them—and feeding Cookie with the bottle has made her special to me, Mom." Zoe smiled proudly. "I got her to take some puppy food and milk in a bowl this morning. Aunt Jo was really happy—she said that she'd thought Cookie was going to have to be on bottles forever!"

"Your Aunt Jo should be paying you!" Mom sighed. "I know you love it at the rescue, but maybe you should have a couple of days off from helping out. Do something else. I bet Kyla could take a break from studying to take you shopping. Or to the movies?"

Zoe looked horrified. "Oh, no, Mom! I have to keep going. I have to help Cookie learn to eat the solid food. It's really important."

Her mom gave her a worried look. "Well, I guess so...."

Chapter Five
Becca's Visit

"It sounds like the best Easter vacation ever!" Becca sighed enviously.

Zoe smiled at her as they walked into their classroom. "It was awesome. I really missed going to the rescue this morning. I was looking forward to seeing you, but aside from that, I could have done without school!"

"Me, too, but I can't see my mom

letting me have the day off because I needed to go and visit the world's cutest puppies...." Becca flopped down into her chair and glanced at the board. "Multiplication problems! Great start to the new quarter...." She got out her math book but went on talking in a whisper. "So is Cookie completely weaned now? She's eating real puppy food?"

Zoe nodded. "Yup, they all still drink a little bit of milk, but they've started drinking water, too. And Cookie's really catching up with Brownie and Chip. I don't think she'll ever be as big as they are, but she's doing okay. I brought the pictures Mom printed out—I'll show you at recess—Shhh! Mrs. Allen is watching us." She stopped talking and tried to look like she was concentrating on the problems that Mrs. Allen had put on the board for them. Their teacher was usually a lot of fun, but she always got extra strict when they came back after vacation—as though she thought they needed to remember what school was like!

Zoe showed the pictures to Becca and some of the other girls in her class at recess, and everyone said how adorable the puppies were. Several of the girls said they were going to ask their moms and dads if they could come to the rescue and see the puppies, and maybe even adopt one of them. Zoe knew that most of her friends wouldn't be allowed to—Lucy already had two dogs at home! But the more people who came to see the puppies, the better. As much as Zoe hated the thought of the puppies leaving the rescue, she wanted them to have the very best homes.

That afternoon, Aunt Jo had arranged to pick Zoe up from school. Mom was going to get her after she finished work. Zoe got changed quickly in the bathroom—Mom hated it when she got her school uniform dirty—and then ran to see Cookie and the others.

Cookie was curled up in their basket, watching her brothers playing tug-of-war with a piece of old rope that someone had given them. They'd had it since the morning, and it was their new favorite toy. Pieces of it were scattered all over the pen. She sighed a little and rested her nose on her paws, wondering where Zoe was. Zoe had played with her every day since they'd come here from their old home. Actually, the little puppy couldn't remember much of where they'd lived before they'd been at the rescue. The only thing she was sure of was that their mother had been at the old place. She still wondered what had happened, and why they had been taken away, but she didn't mind, because now she had Zoe.

Except that today she didn't, and she didn't understand why. Zoe always fed her and her brothers. Zoe gave them a lot of attention, even though she wasn't feeding milk from her lap anymore. Zoe still brought the food bowls and watched to make sure that she was eating enough. Zoe even stopped Brownie and Chip from trying to take her food if they finished theirs first.

Today the other lady had brought their food—Jo, the one who was always with Zoe. Jo had said nice things, and she'd petted her, and said how good she was. But it wasn't the same.

Cookie's little ears pricked up sharply. Someone was running along the hallway between the pens—someone with small, light footsteps. She jumped up in the basket and barked excitedly as Zoe appeared at the front of the pen, beaming at her.

"Oh! Did you miss me? I really missed you," Zoe told her, opening the latch. "You too, yes, I missed you as well, you great big monsters," she told Brownie and Chip, patting them lovingly as they circled around her feet. But it was Cookie that she sat down next to, and Cookie she cuddled as soon as the puppy clambered happily into her lap.

"I missed you more," Zoe whispered into her ears as she petted her. "I know I shouldn't really say it, but I did." She sighed. "There are some people who are going to come and look at you, Cookie. Try to look like a perfect pet, okay? You aren't old enough to go for a couple more weeks, but if they like you, they might wait."

She could hear them coming along the line of pens now—a couple, who'd just bought a house together, and were thinking of getting a dog. They'd said they didn't mind whether it was a puppy or an older dog, but when Aunt Jo had mentioned the three beautiful little puppies, they had gotten excited.

"They'll be looking for you." Zoe sighed again. "They looked nice, I guess. Nice-ish...." She couldn't imagine anyone being a good enough owner for her special Cookie. No one except her, she realized with a miserable little gulp.

"So they decided on Jasper?" Zoe asked as she helped her aunt to clean out the food bowls, feeling a bit surprised, but very relieved. Jasper was about five years old and was a mixed-breed, mostly Labrador. *He isn't as cute as Cookie and her brothers*, Zoe thought.

"Yes, they decided that they wanted a bigger dog after all," Aunt Jo explained. "Don't worry, Zoe. It won't be hard to find homes for those three at all. They're beautiful. It's the older dogs that can be hard to place."

Zoe nodded. "My friend Becca is going to get a dog soon. Becca said she'd love to come and see the puppies. She's going to ask her mom and dad if they could come this weekend. That would be okay, wouldn't it?" Her voice wobbled a little bit. "It'll only be one more week until the puppies are old enough to go to new homes then...."

Aunt Jo looked closely at her. "Yes, they'll be about seven weeks old this weekend, as far as we can tell. It won't hurt them to be split up from their litter after eight weeks. It would be wonderful for one of your friends to come. Zoe, are you okay, sweetheart?"

"I'll miss them, that's all," Zoe muttered.

"I know you will. Especially Cookie. You've taken care of her so well. But she can't stay here, Zo, you know that. It isn't a good life for a dog, in a little pen like this, no matter much we love them."

"I know. But it's hard to think of someone else taking her home. I wish we could have a dog! I'd take care of her so well!" Zoe burst out. Then she added quietly, "Don't worry, I know we can't...."

Aunt Jo hugged her, accidentally clanging two stainless steel dishes together behind her back, and making Zoe laugh.

"I'm so excited!" Becca raced up the steps toward Zoe, her mom following behind. She flung her arms around her. "Please can we see all the dogs? And the cats? I know we don't want a cat, but I'd like to see them anyway. And the guinea pigs!"

"I'll show you everything," Zoe promised, giggling. She hadn't seen her friend so hyper since her birthday party. She took them all around the rescue, saving the dog pens until last.

"You're so lucky, getting to help here all the time," Becca told her, cooing at the guinea pigs. Then she looked excitedly up at her mom. "Please can you show us the dogs now, Zoe? Mom and Dad said we might be able to get one really soon. That's what Dad's doing today—fixing our fence so that there aren't any holes around the bottom of it, and it's safe for a dog to be in the yard. He said if we found a dog from

73

somewhere like here, the rescue would want to come and check that we'd take care of it well."

Zoe nodded. "Yes, Aunt Jo and the other staff go and look around everyone's houses. They wouldn't let you have a cat from here if you lived on a really busy road. Or if you had small children. You'll be all right," she added. "You want a dog, and it's only really small children that are a problem—you know, too small to understand about not pulling tails."

Becca nodded.

"Doesn't your dad want to help choose a dog?" Zoe asked curiously.

Becca's mom smiled. "This is just a first look—so we can think about what kind of dog we'd like. Becca's dad will come and see them if we tell him there's a dog we really like. But he started worrying about the fence last night, and he was determined to get it done. He didn't want us to miss out on a beautiful dog because the house wasn't ready."

Zoe smiled. It sounded as though Becca and her mom and dad were really serious about getting a dog. They weren't just deciding to adopt one without thinking it through, like some people did. "Okay, well, here are the dog pens. It can get pretty noisy!" she warned Becca, as several of the dogs started to bark excitedly when they realized they had visitors.

"Oh, look...," Becca whispered, glancing from side to side. "So many!

Lulu, Freddie…. Oh, he's so handsome! Mom, look! He looks like a German shepherd. Oooh! Trixie!" Becca crouched down by the little spaniel's pen. "She's so pretty…."

She glanced up worriedly at Zoe. "How do people ever choose? She's looking at me, like she really wants us to take her home, and I haven't even gone halfway along the pens yet!"

"It is hard," Zoe admitted. "If you think you really like any of the dogs, tell me, and I'll ask Aunt Jo if you can go into the pens and meet them."

"If I did that, I'd never be able to say no," Becca's mom muttered. "What if we cuddled a dog and then said we didn't want him? It would be heartbreaking!"

Zoe wrinkled her nose. She supposed she was more used to the rescue than most people. "I know it's sad. But Aunt Jo and the others do find homes for all the dogs in the end. It takes a while for some of them, though." She led Becca and her mom along the row of pens. "And these…," she stopped by a pen, "are the puppies we found abandoned."

She laughed as all three of them raced toward the wire of the pen. "The one with the darker brown patches is Brownie, and that one's Chip...." She pointed to the puppy with the brown eyepatch. "And this one, with the pale brown patches," she paused, "is Cookie."

"Oh, wow...," Becca sighed. "They're all so beautiful!"

"They are adorable," her mom agreed. "They look very little, Zoe. Are they old enough to be adopted?"

"Not for about another week," Zoe explained. "But then it will be fine, although they still can't go outside for a while after that. All the dogs in here have been vaccinated, but puppies have to have more vaccinations when they're about 12 weeks old. Then they can go for walks. They'd be okay in the yard, though," she added.

"You know a lot about dogs," Becca said admiringly. "Can we pet them? Mom, do you want to?"

Her mom nodded, smiling. "Definitely."

Zoe swallowed hard and opened the latch on the pen. It was a good thing that Becca and her mom liked the puppies. But it was one step closer to them leaving the rescue ... and Zoe.

Cookie scratched excitedly at the wire. Zoe had been playing with them that morning, and then she'd disappeared. Now she was back!

But there were other people, too. Another girl, like Zoe, and someone else. Cookie had never seen them before. She stopped wagging her tail quite so hard and backed up a bit as Zoe opened the door. She wasn't used to different people.

Zoe let Becca and her mom in, and Brownie and Chip sniffed cautiously at them. Becca picked up the last piece of the rope toy and wiggled it along the ground, right in front of Brownie, who quickly pounced on it, pretending to growl.

"He's so funny!" Becca giggled.

"I think he's the friendliest of the puppies," Zoe told her. She looked around for Cookie, who was almost hiding behind her, watching Becca and her mom with big, anxious eyes. "It's all right, Cookie," she whispered.

Cookie pressed herself against Zoe's side and sniffed cautiously at Becca's mom's fingers when she held them out. The new people smelled nice, but she didn't know them like she knew Zoe. She didn't mind if this lady petted her, though.

"She's very sweet," Becca's mom said. "Is this the one you bottle-fed, Zoe? You can see that she adores you."

Zoe smiled sadly. She loved that Cookie acted like her dog, even though she wasn't. She sighed. Cookie was going to have to learn to love somebody else. Gently, she lifted Cookie up and put her on Becca's mom's lap.

Cookie froze and sat motionless, her shoulders all hunched up under her ears. She looked around at Zoe worriedly, but she didn't wriggle off. It was all right. Zoe was still there, very close. The lady rubbed her ears, which was nice. She relaxed a little, and licked her hand.

"She's a tiny bit shy, but she's very loving," Zoe said, trying not to mind someone else cuddling Cookie. She took a deep breath. "She'd be a wonderful pet. Any of them would."

Cookie watched sadly, her ears
flattening back, as they all got up. They
were going, she could tell. She missed Zoe
so much now that she didn't stay all day
the way she used to. Zoe had been here
for longer today, but Cookie still hadn't
had her snack. Cookie liked it when Zoe
brought her food and sat with her while
she ate. She always ate more when Zoe
was there, because Zoe liked to see her

eat, and she would tell her what a good dog she was, eating so nicely.

As Zoe was shutting the front of the pen, Cookie raced after her, scratching her claws against the wire netting and whining sadly.

"It's okay," Zoe whispered to her. "I'll be back tomorrow. I promise."

Cookie didn't know what that meant, but she understood Zoe's comforting voice. She stopped whining and just stood up against the wire, staring after the girls as they walked down the hallway between the pens. She watched until the doors swung shut and she couldn't see Zoe anymore. Then she dropped down and sadly padded over to their basket, her claws clicking against the worn tiles on the floor.

Chapter Six
A Difficult Week

"Mom says we can make pancakes for dinner!" Becca told Zoe happily as they took their coats off.

"I love pancakes," Zoe said, trying to sound more cheerful than she felt. It was a treat to go to Becca's house, but she would have preferred to stay at the shelter with Cookie and the others for a little longer. It would be rude to say that, though.

The girls curled up on the couch and watched a movie. Zoe was careful not to let herself think about how nice it would be if there were a little puppy snuggled up between them watching, too. But next time, there might be. Becca's dad was still outside fixing the fence. When they'd gotten back, he'd shown them the shiny new wire neatly running around the base of the old wooden fence. They'd taken him out a cup of tea and a plate of cookies, and he'd said gratefully that he thought he was almost finished. It looked like their entire family was really committed to having a dog.

Becca had gone to get them both some juice, leaving Zoe watching the movie—they'd both seen it before—

and now she came running back in.

"Zoe! I've just been talking to Mom and Dad, and guess what!"

Zoe blinked at her in surprise.

"We're going to ask your aunt if we can reserve one of the three puppies! Mom's calling her now! She's arranging for them to come and do a home visit, too!" Becca was dancing around the room in delight, and Zoe stared at her.

This was good news. One of the puppies was going to have a wonderful new home and be well taken care of. Zoe would even be able to keep on seeing whichever puppy they chose. She'd know what the puppies would look like when they were grown up, after all!

But what if they choose Cookie? the voice inside Zoe's head whispered. Then Cookie would belong to someone else. She stopped herself. This was her best friend, Becca, that they were talking about. Cookie would have a perfect home.

"That's wonderful," she told Becca finally, swallowing back the lump in her throat. "Aunt Jo will be really happy."

"Oh, and Mom says dinner is ready," Becca added.

Zoe nodded. That was good. After dinner, it would be time for her to go home, and she wouldn't have to keep pretending to be happy for Becca. She knew that she should be, but she wasn't.

She was burningly, horribly jealous instead, and she felt terrible for it.

"We went out yesterday to that big pet store over by the supermarket. Have you ever been there?"

Zoe shook her head.

"I hadn't, either. It's enormous, and it sells everything! You'd love it, Zoe," Becca rambled on happily. "Your aunt emailed Mom a long list of stuff we'll need, and we even got some things that weren't on the list, just because they were so fun! Lots of toys! The puppies love playing with those toys they have in their pen at the rescue, don't they?"

Zoe nodded. "Yes," she muttered quietly, burying her head as she took her pencil case and book out of her bag.

"And we have to make sure that our puppy has a lot to do, because it might be lonely without any others to play with. Although I'll be there, of course. Zoe, are you okay?" Becca added. "You're so quiet."

"I'm fine." Zoe tried to sound enthusiastic. "Did you get a rope toy? The puppies really like that old piece of rope they've got."

"Yes! A beautiful one. Much nicer than that ratty old one they have now."

Zoe sniffed, trying not to cry. *But they like that ratty old piece of rope,* she thought to herself. *And what if Becca chooses Cookie?* Zoe stopped herself. Whichever puppy Becca chose was going to be so lucky.

I'd be a good owner, too, she said to herself miserably. *I know so much about taking care of dogs. I've fed those puppies, and cleaned up after them, and washed them when they got themselves covered in puppy food....*

"Did you hear me, Zoe?" Becca nudged her gently, and Zoe jumped.

"Um, no. I'm sorry. What?"

"I just said that we're going to go to the rescue on Saturday and choose the puppy, and then it can come home with us!"

"Oh!" *So soon!* Zoe swallowed hard. "That's great," she muttered. "Um, I'm going to the bathroom. Tell Mrs. Allen where I am if she comes, okay?"

Zoe tried as hard as she could to be her usual self with Becca that week, but it was so, so difficult.

Becca clearly knew that something was wrong. Zoe kept avoiding her, and dashing off to change her library book instead of chatting with Becca and their other friends at lunchtime. She spent the entire recess hiding in the bathroom one day after Becca started telling her about the beautiful collars she'd seen on a pet website. They had little pawprint designs woven into them, and space for a phone number, so that if the dog got lost it was easy for someone to call you. It had just made Zoe feel too upset. She'd had to tell Becca she felt sick when the bell rang.

Zoe hated lying to her friend all the time, but she didn't want to admit how jealous and nasty she was really feeling.

By Friday, Becca had stopped telling her about all the things they were doing to get ready for the puppy. She almost wasn't talking to Zoe at all. And at lunch she went off and played with a group of other girls in their class, without even asking Zoe if she wanted to join in.

"See you tomorrow morning, then," she told Zoe rather awkwardly as they put their coats on at the end of the day.

Zoe nodded. "Okay. 'Bye, Becca."

And that was that. No running out to the gate together. No promises to call later about homework. Becca just walked away, leaving Zoe fiddling with the zipper on her jacket and feeling totally miserable.

Kyla was waiting for her outside school as usual—the high school was just up the road from Zoe's school, and she usually got out later than Zoe did, but Zoe had taken a long time that afternoon.

"Are you all right?" she asked. "You look really down."

Zoe shrugged. "I'm sort of not talking to Becca," she admitted. "It's horrible."

"Did you have a fight?" her sister asked sympathetically.

"No." Zoe sighed. "It's all my fault. You know the puppies at the rescue?"

Kyla laughed. "No, Zoe, it's not as if you've ever talked about them at home."

Zoe swung her schoolbag at her sister, making a face. But Kyla was always good at cheering her up. "She's going to adopt one."

Kyla smiled, and then looked confused. "But that's good, isn't it?"

"Yes," Zoe said in a small voice. "I just wish I could, too, that's all. I'm jealous…. And worse than that, I'm worried that she might choose Cookie."

"Oh, Zo…." Kyla hugged her. "I haven't met these puppies, but I can see how much they mean to you.

Why don't we stop off at the rescue so you can show me them?"

"But you hate dogs!" Zoe stared at her.

"I don't hate them." Kyla shrugged. "I think I'm getting better. One of my friends at school has a really cute spaniel. I even let him sit on my lap on the couch the other day."

"Wow, Kyla! That's great!" Zoe smiled. "Of course I'll show you the puppies. You're going to love them, especially Cookie—she's beautiful. I was going to ask Mom if she could take me over there later, but let's go now." She grabbed Kyla's hand and practically pulled her down the road.

"All right, all right, take it easy!" Kyla grinned.

It didn't take them long to walk across

the park toward Redwood, and soon they were turning into the driveway.

"I brought Kyla to see the puppies!" she told Aunt Jo as they popped their heads around the office door.

Aunt Jo looked up from her computer. "Hi, Kyla!" She grinned. "That's great news."

"Hi, Aunt Jo." Kyla smiled back. "I just thought I'd like to see them. Mom said they were really cute."

"They are." Aunt Jo nodded. "I'll call your mom and tell her you're both here. I can take you home in the car if you'd like."

"That would be great," said Zoe. "Come on, Kyla—they're down here." Zoe grabbed Kyla's hand and pulled her down the hallway. "Don't worry. I don't think there are any really big dogs in the rescue at the moment," she added, seeing her sister glancing cautiously into the pens.

"I just don't like it when they jump against the wire," Kyla whispered.

"Brownie and Chip do jump up, but they're really little," Zoe promised. "Cookie won't, not until she's figured out who you are, because she's a little shy."

"Okay. Oh, Zoe, are these them?" Kyla stopped in front of the puppies' pen, smiling at them delightedly. They were all asleep, for once, flopped in a sort of puppy pile in their basket. The pile heaved and wriggled every so often, and as Zoe gently undid the front of the pen, the pile struggled apart and turned into three hairy, whiskery, brown and white puppies who bounced happily around Zoe's feet.

"Do you want me to bring one of the puppies out?" Zoe asked. "Then you could pet just one—you wouldn't have them jumping all over you."

Kyla nodded, and Zoe picked Cookie up. Cookie nuzzled at her happily. She'd been hoping that Zoe would come soon. She looked around curiously as Zoe carried her out of the pen, leaving her two brothers behind, looking rather jealous. Cookie stared down at them, wagging her stubby little tail.

Zoe was carrying her to another girl, a taller girl with the same dark hair and eyes. Cookie looked at her with her head to one side—she looked very much like Zoe. But she didn't seem to be confident with dogs the way that Zoe was. She was looking nervous, and as she put out her hand, she patted her very quickly, as if she thought Cookie might bite.

Curious about this girl who looked so much like her favorite person, Cookie wriggled in Zoe's arms, stretching toward the other girl.

"She likes you!" Zoe said laughing.

"Does she?" Kyla asked, sounding surprised, and happy.

"Yes, she does," said Zoe. "Do you want to hold her?"

"I don't know...." Kyla looked uncertain. "Okay, let me try."

Kyla nodded slowly, then let Zoe put Cookie into her arms.

Cookie snuggled up against Kyla's chin, and slowly, Kyla petted her ears. The little dog closed her eyes.

"Oh, Zoe, she's beautiful." Kyla smiled down at the puppy. "No wonder you've been spending so much time here."

"She is, isn't she?" Zoe sighed sadly. "And now I just can't bear to think of letting her go...."

Chapter Seven
Decision Time

Cookie scampered around on the grass, chasing after the jingly ball. It was her favorite toy. She loved the noise it made, even though she didn't quite understand where the noise came from. It was definitely hers—Zoe had given it to her. It was the only toy she bothered to fight over.

Chip raced past her and dove onto

the ball, rolling over with it with his paws, and growling excitedly.

Cookie let out a sharp, furious bark and jumped on top of him, scrambling to get the ball back. Unfortunately, Chip was still quite a bit bigger than she was, and he wriggled and growled. Then somehow he was sitting on top of her instead, and he had the ball, in his teeth now. He shook it backward and forward, still growling, so that it jingled like crazy.

"Stop fighting you two!" Zoe ran over. "Chip, Chip, look! Stretchy bone! Your best bone! Come on! Where's it going?"

Chip sprang up, dropping the ball, and danced around in circles as Zoe waved the blue rubber bone. Then she flung it across the yard, and he galloped after it like a racehorse.

Cookie seized her ball gratefully and sat down on Zoe's feet, panting.

"You really love that ball, don't you?" Zoe reached down and picked her up. "Look, there's a nice sunny patch over there. Let's just sit and watch those two brothers of yours being silly...."

It was a beautiful, warm May day, and Zoe had shorts on for the first time that year. She should have been feeling happy, but all she could think about was Becca. She'd be here soon. Which puppy would she choose? Zoe ran her hand gently down Cookie's back, over and over, as Cookie shook the ball gently back and forth, listening to the jingly noises.

"What if she chooses you, Cookie?" Zoe whispered. "I've been trying not to think about it. It was bad enough just thinking about Becca having a dog, and me not being able to have one. But what if it's actually you that she wants to take home with her?" She sighed and leaned over, resting her cheek against Cookie's soft fur for a moment. "At least I'd still get to see you. That's if Becca ever talks to me again, considering the way I've been acting this week. I've been awful."

Cookie looked at her for a moment, her eyes dark and sparkly. She licked Zoe's hand.

"Thank you!" Zoe grinned. "Was that to tell me you don't think I've been awful? I have, though. I was horrible, actually. I just can't tell if it would be worse to never see you again, or to see that you belong to someone else! I don't know whether to hope that Becca chooses you or not." This time Zoe heaved a massive sigh, so that Cookie turned around and stared at her. "I'm sorry! Did I shake you up and down?"

"Zoe!" Aunt Jo was calling her. "Becca and her mom and dad are here! They're just getting out of their car. Go and say hello. I'll bring these three in."

"Oh! Okay." Zoe gently put Cookie down, and the puppy scampered off after the ball again. She walked slowly through the rescue to the reception area, where Becca and her parents were now talking to Susie, who was at the reception desk.

"You two can chat while we fill out the paperwork," Becca's mom told them, smiling.

Becca couldn't have told her mom how grumpy Zoe had been all week, Zoe realized gratefully. "Hi…," she said timidly to Becca.

"Hi." Becca stared at her, and then

she pulled Zoe over into the corner, as if they were going to look at photos on the wall of the dogs and cats who'd been adopted recently. "Zoe, is there something going on?" she asked. "Are you mad at me?"

Zoe turned red and looked at her feet. "No … I…." She didn't know what to say.

"You are!" Becca cried out. "You've been acting really weird all week! What is it? What have I done?"

Zoe sighed. "Nothing. Nothing at all. I know I've been acting weird, but it isn't your fault. It's me. I've been jealous … jealous because you were getting a dog, and I couldn't have one, not ever. We don't have anyone at home to take care of a dog, and Kyla hates them anyway. I'm so sorry I've been horrible."

"Oh, Zoe." Becca gave her friend a big hug. "Why didn't you tell me?" she asked her, stepping back, her eyes round with surprise. "I'd have understood!"

"I suppose I just felt silly. And mean," Zoe muttered. "And I didn't really want to talk to you about it. You were so excited...."

Becca sighed. "I didn't think about it making you sad," she admitted. "Did I go on and on?"

Zoe gave a very small giggle. "Yes. All the time."

A voice behind them interrupted the awkward moment. It was Becca's dad.

"Are you girls ready?" he asked them. "I want to see these wonderful puppies you've been telling me about!"

Becca looked anxiously at Zoe, but Zoe nodded, managing to smile and look almost as though she meant it. "Come on!"

They walked down the hallway to the puppies' pen. Zoe spotted Aunt Jo coming back in from the yard with the puppies in her arms. "There they are," she told Becca's dad, pointing. "They've been playing outside."

The puppies saw them, too, and started to wriggle excitedly. Aunt Jo laughed and crouched down, letting them run down the hallway toward the visitors.

Cookie dashed ahead, streaking toward Zoe on her tiny little legs. Zoe was desperate to pick her up and cuddle her. But she couldn't. It was Becca's turn.

But Becca wasn't looking at Cookie, Zoe realized. She'd crouched down and was holding out her arms. Chip was running straight up to her, and now he was standing up on his hind legs, his front paws on her arms, giving happy, excited little barks. He licked her cheek and jumped, as though she was the best thing he'd ever seen!

"He remembers me!" Becca cried delightedly. "I've only met him once, but he really remembers me! Oh, Dad, do you like him? His name is Chip, and he's the best one of all. Can we please take him home?"

Chapter Eight
Cookie's Perfect Home

Zoe watched, smiling, as Becca hugged Chip. He wriggled delightedly in her arms. So it would be a stranger who would be taking Cookie home, she realized sadly. She wouldn't see her adorable little puppy grow up into a beautiful dog after all.

Cookie patted her paws hopefully at Zoe's leg, asking to be picked up.

She could tell that Zoe was sad, but Cookie knew that she could make her feel better. When Zoe lifted her up at last, Cookie stood up in her arms, rubbing her whiskery nose against Zoe's cheek. That always made her laugh.

"You're so pretty," Zoe told her, but she didn't sound much happier.

Cookie watched interestedly as the girl cuddling Chip gave him some crunchy treats, and carefully lifted him into a box, which was like a small pen with a wire front. She shivered a little, burying her nose in Zoe's neck. It reminded her of the box they'd all been closed up in. It felt like a very long time ago now.

Chip looked confused, and whined, but the girl fed him some more treats through the wire, and then the man with her picked the box up and carried him away down the hall to the door.

Cookie gave a little whimper of

surprise. They could go away? Chip was going with that girl, and the other two people? She didn't understand. If they were allowed out of the rescue, why didn't Zoe take her when she went? Maybe she would! Maybe they were all going! Cookie's tail started to flick back and forth with excitement.

"Well, that was good, wasn't it?" Aunt Jo said, sounding really happy. "And I meant to tell you, Zoe, a really nice-sounding family called me asking about puppies, and they were interested in getting a boy puppy—so that would be you, Brownie." She looked down at the puppy in her arms, who'd barked when he heard his name. "Yes, you! They're going to come and see you tomorrow, aren't they, sweetie? So we're getting there."

Zoe nodded. So that would leave just Cookie. And she wouldn't be there for much longer either, Zoe was sure.

"Oh, look, there's your mom and Kyla," Aunt Jo pointed out, and she turned to open the front of the pen and put Brownie back in.

Zoe sighed, and walked toward the pen to put Cookie in, too. She'd forgotten that Mom was coming to pick her up early. She wanted them to go and do some shopping—Zoe needed new school shoes. Zoe had tried arguing that Mom could just buy them for her, but Mom had said no.

Cookie twisted in her arms, struggling frantically, and whining. She wasn't going back in the pen—she wanted to stay with Zoe! Someone had already taken Chip away. Only Zoe could take her.

"What's the matter?" Zoe gasped, holding the puppy tightly, and backing away from the pen, as that seemed to be what was upsetting her.

"Is Cookie okay?" Mom asked worriedly. She and Kyla had just come into the hallway between the pens, and now she was hurrying toward Zoe.

"She got really upset when I was trying to put her back in the pen." Zoe cuddled Cookie close against her shoulder. She could feel the little dog's sides heaving; she was shaking so badly. "Maybe she's sad about Chip going." She wrinkled up her brow.

"It's okay, Cookie. It's okay," she whispered. But then her eyes filled with tears. "I'm telling her everything's going to be all right, but it isn't," she said miserably, looking between Aunt Jo and Mom. "Chip has gone to a new home, and Brownie will probably go, too, tomorrow, and then it'll be just Cookie left. And someone will choose her really soon, and we'll never see her again."

Aunt Jo frowned. "I wonder if she does know what's happening. Some dogs really do seem to understand, far more than you'd think they could. Maybe that's why she doesn't want to go back into that pen."

"But she has to," Zoe said dismally. "What are we going to do? Do you think she'd be better if we moved her into a different pen?"

Aunt Jo glanced at Mom and shook her head. "No, to be honest, I think it would just be better if she went back with you."

"But then it would just be harder for her to come back here." Zoe blinked, not really understanding what her aunt was saying.

"Or we could keep her," her mom said, putting an arm around Zoe's shoulders and gently patting Cookie.

Zoe looked puzzled. "But there's no one to take care of her in the daytime."

Her mom glanced at Aunt Jo. "We've been talking about that. I told your aunt I was worried about how much you were falling in love with Cookie. That you were going to be really upset when she went to her new home."

"And I said you were so good with dogs that you really deserved to have one of your own," said Aunt Jo.

"So we've come up with a plan," said her mom.

"I'm going to have her here at work with me in the day, Zoe," Aunt Jo explained. "She can have a basket under my desk, and I'll take her for a walk at lunchtime."

"And Kyla?" said Zoe, flashing her

sister a look.

"I don't feel scared around Cookie," said Kyla. "She's a little sweetheart. Mom told me how much you'd bonded with Cookie—it was actually my idea that we should have her. That's why I wanted to meet her last week."

"Really?" Zoe stared at them all, her eyes like saucers. "You mean it? We can have Cookie? So—so we could take her home now?" Zoe whispered, hardly daring to hope that they'd say yes.

Aunt Jo smiled. "Well, she obviously doesn't want to go back in that pen. I can stay here and give Brownie a lot of attention so he doesn't mind being on his own. And you can borrow some food bowls and things, until you can get your own."

Zoe nodded, thinking how much allowance money she had saved up, and how she was going to spend all of it at the pet store on the little puppy. Cookie was going to have the nicest things she could find.

"You're coming home with us," she

whispered to Cookie. "You really are."

Cookie nudged Zoe's cheek with her damp black nose and looked hopefully at the door.

"Look at them! They're having such a good time," Zoe said, laughing at the two little brown and white dogs—Chip and Cookie. Who would have thought it? They were standing at the bottom of a huge tree, right at the end of their extending leashes. And they were both jumping up and down, barking like crazy.

"I wonder if Brownie likes chasing squirrels, too," Becca said thoughtfully. "Maybe we'll see him in the park one of these days."

Zoe nodded. "I bet he does. And I bet he never catches them, either."

The squirrel was sitting high up in the tree now, looking down at the two dogs in disgust. They hadn't come anywhere near getting him, and he clearly wasn't very bothered. He almost looked like he was yawning.

Eventually, Cookie and Chip gave up on the squirrel and wandered back to Zoe and Becca.

"Cookie's catching up with him," Becca commented. "She's almost as big as he is now. She might even end up being bigger!"

"Maybe," Zoe agreed. "They probably won't finish growing until they're about nine months old. Maybe even a year. They're four months old now, so they've got five months more growing to do, at least. You're going to be a huge dog one day, aren't you?" she told Cookie affectionately, crouching down and rubbing her ears and petting her back.

Becca giggled. Cookie might get bigger one day, but she and Chip were still tiny at the moment. Not that they seemed to think they were little at all. They strutted through the park as though they thought they were the most important dogs there.

"They wouldn't fit in that box now," Zoe said suddenly, looking up at Becca.

Becca shook her head. "I still don't know how someone could have left them like that. But I'm just glad it was you and your Aunt Jo who found them."

Zoe nodded, scratching Cookie under the chin, so that she closed her eyes blissfully, and her tail thumped on the ground.

"I know. Me, too."